JUDY'S SUMMER FRIEND
by
Elizabeth Ladd

Illustrated by Mary Stevens

Judy knew the "summer people" were different from the people who lived in Maine all year, although she looked forward to meeting a girl her own age who was coming to Cape Oregon for the season. Laurel's flashy sailboat arrived before she did, and made Judy's borrowed punt look shabby. Laurel also picked a fight with David, who owned a boat called *North Wind* which he used to fish for a living, and Judy didn't know whose side to take. The girls did have fun together but the tension between the summer visitors and those who lived in Maine still remained. The mysterious and nearly disastrous disappearance of David's fishing boat brought things to a head between the two girls and David.

* * *

Classification and Dewey Decimal: Fiction (Fic)

About the Author:

ELIZABETH LADD was born in Maine and brought up on the island of Islesboro in the Penobscot Bay. She was an only child with few playmates and many pets. She began to write at an early age, determined to be an author. After a brief stay at the University of Maine she returned to Islesboro where she shared with her father the work and planning of their farm. All of Miss Ladd's books present a vivid picture of life on the Maine coast.

About the Illustrator:

MARY STEVENS spent her childhood in Bar Harbor, Maine. She attended art school in Boston and New York. Both her father and grandfather were artistic and she recalls that her father's bedtime stories always were accompanied with illustrations on a blackboard. Miss Stevens does volunteer work at a cancer hospital and explores the little-known backstreets of every borough in New York. She spends a good deal of time at Bar Harbor, because she feels lonesome when she is too far from the sea.

Judy's Summer Friend

Judy's

Summer Friend

by ELIZABETH LADD

Illustrated by MARY STEVENS

1966 FIRST CADMUS EDITION
THIS SPECIAL EDITION IS PUBLISHED BY ARRANGEMENT WITH
THE PUBLISHERS OF THE REGULAR EDITION
WILLIAM MORROW & CO. INC.
BY
E. M. HALE AND COMPANY
EAU CLAIRE, WISCONSIN

Contents

CHAPTER 1

The Quarrel

Bundled warm in her winter clothes, Judy walked slowly down the path toward the old wharf. Winter was growing old, but a thin covering of snow still lay over the frozen land. Through the leafless birches the mountains behind Summerport loomed up, icy blue. Along the shore slabs of salt-water ice, soft and spongy, like cakes of creamy fudge, were stacked up above the tide line. The tide was ebbing, and the rockweed and the bare mud flats were

black as ink against the snow on the banking.

Judy had to walk slowly, she had on so many clothes—her wool jacket, snow pants, rubber overshoes, and the red mittens and the scarf that her Aunt Kate had knitted for her. She drew the warm scarf across her face, for the north wind cut like a ragged knife whenever it touched flesh.

The old lobster boat that belonged to her Uncle Walter was lying beside the wharf. Judy could already see the tip of its mast rising above the end of the wharf. Judy's home was with her aunt and uncle on their farm in Maine, and during the summer Uncle Walter used the boat to set lobster traps around Cape Oregon, a point of land which stuck out into the sea. In winter it was too cold to go lobstering, so Uncle Walter fitted the old boat for scallop dragging instead.

The part of the winter that Judy liked the best was scallop-dragging time. Mr. Young, who lived next door and who was the father of Judy's best friend, David, went in the boat with Uncle Walter. They were up and away long before daylight, long before Judy left for school, and they came home late at night. Then they still had to shuck the scallops and take them in to the market at Summerport before they were finished with their day's work.

Sometimes Uncle Walter would bring home a bucket of scallops for their own use. No matter how often they had them to eat, Judy felt she could never tire of scallops. Aunt Kate rolled them in cracker crumbs and fried them in pork fat until they were golden brown. When you ate them you could taste the goodness of the scallop and the sweetness of the pork fat on the back of your tongue. Sometimes Aunt Kate poured hot milk and melted butter over the freshly cooked scallops and made a delicious stew with them. Uncle Walter said that it "just hit the spot," when he came in out of the winter's cold.

Her uncle had taught Judy to eat scallops raw, although Aunt Kate would have none of them. Judy thought they were the best this way; they almost melted in her mouth and they had the faintest salty taste of the sea about them. She was really lucky, Judy thought, to live in a place where there were so many kinds of wonderful things to eat, like scallops and flounders and lobsters.

Judy had seen the big drag when it was taken out of the barn in the fall and examined for holes. The drag looked like a giant pocketbook made of chain with a mouth of steel bars. A rope or a chain would be fastened to it, and then it would be dropped overboard and towed behind the boat. The boat would go along very slowly, scraping the drag over the bottom of the sea. Anything in its way—rocks, shells, fish, or scallops—would be scooped up inside of it. When it became heavy it would be pulled to the surface by a small derrick, and the contents would be dumped into the boat. Then it would be lowered for a new drag while the men picked out and threw away all the rocks, rubbish, and worthless things that they had dragged up. They kept the fish if they were good to eat, and, of course, the scallops. But you could not drag just anywhere over the bottom and expect to get scallops, any more than you could set a lobster trap just anywhere and

expect to catch a lobster. Scallops lived together in what were called beds. Mr. Young
and Uncle Walter knew just where these beds
were, and they would drag back and forth
across them. Even so, sometimes they would
get a dragful of scallops and sometimes only
a handful.

Then the scallops had to be shucked, like
clams, before they could be eaten. The shells
were cut open with a knife, but, unlike a clam,
only a small part of the scallop was saved. The
big white muscle that held the shell halves together was cut out and the rest of the scallop
was thrown away. Gulls fought for the scraps,
and scallop boats, like herring boats, often had
a trail of gulls behind them.

On Saturdays, when he was free from school,
David went with the men. Judy had asked if
she couldn't go too, but Uncle Walter had made
all sorts of excuses. They stayed out too long
and the weather was too cold for a little girl.

Judy didn't think either of these reasons was very good; the boat had a warm cabin with a little stove. If David could stay out in a boat all day she certainly could. David was only a year older. Then Aunt Kate had explained to her that scalloping was something only men and boys do. They liked to be off by themselves and away from womenfolks for a while, and little girls weren't expected to go along.

Boys have all the fun, Judy thought glumly, as she tramped down onto the wharf. Some of the scallop gear needed to be repaired, so although the men and David were aboard the boat they had not gone out today. Judy hoped that they would let her stand on the wharf, or maybe come aboard the boat and watch them work, even if she couldn't go out with them.

David was the only person in sight; he was cleaning odd trash out of the cockpit. He didn't invite her to come aboard, so Judy leaned over the wharf railing to talk with him.

"Soon it'll be time to paint the *Pant*," Judy said, just to make conversation. The *Panther Eye* was David's punt, the apple of his eye, and every spring he carefully painted it. Judy helped him do it.

David threw a rusty tin can overboard. "I shan't paint her this year," he said in a matter-of-fact tone.

Judy stared at him. "But you've got to paint her, or else she'll leak, and she'll look terrible when we use her this summer."

"I'm not going to use her this summer," David answered. When Judy kept on staring at him, he added, "Didn't you know? Dad's bought the *North Wind,* that big boat over to Summerport. He'll need someone to help handle her when he goes lobstering this summer. She's no little tub like this thing." He cast a scornful glance around him at Uncle Walter's old boat. "I'll be getting real day wages," he boasted.

"But what about the *Pant?*" Judy wailed.

"Oh, I'll leave her on the bank, I guess. I can't be bothered with an old punt."

Judy put the tip of her red mitten into her mouth. "Would you do something for me, David? A favor?"

"What?" David asked, leaning on the rail of the boat.

"Would you ask your father and Uncle Walter if I could come out scalloping with you sometime?"

"I should say not." David made no secret of his indignation. "Scalloping is a man's job."

"Please," Judy said. "You're supposed to be my friend."

"Why don't you ask yourself?"

"I have, and it didn't do any good. But if you asked too, especially your father, maybe it would help. He's the one who doesn't want me to go."

"My father doesn't want to be bothered with a girl," David said.

"Your father's mean and so are you," Judy said spitefully. "And now I suppose you'll be more stuck up than ever with a new boat."

"It's too bad your uncle couldn't have a decent boat like the *North Wind.*"

Judy felt her cheeks burn. She knew her people didn't have as much money as David's folks. Uncle Walter was too old to work as hard as David's father, but there was no need for David to hint at this.

"The *Alice* is a fine boat," she said proudly.

"She's little and old and tubby," David said, looking around the boat. "Everyone knows that your uncle lets money slip through his fingers. That's why he can't afford a really good boat."

"And everyone knows your dad is tight as the bark on a tree!" Judy cried.

Now it was David's face that turned a dull

red. "I don't want you to talk about my folks like that again."

He turned around and went down into the cabin of the *Alice*. Judy stomped off the wharf in a rage. Her anger lasted as far as the shore; then she began to think things over. This was the first time she had ever quarreled with David. Oh, they had had their arguments, but they had been over quickly. Now there had been angry words between them, and they had both said things they didn't mean. Judy wished that she had held her tongue, for she saw that it was much easier to say a word than it was to take it back.

CHAPTER 2

Burning the Fields

Spring was here at last. The snow was gone and the fields of winter grass stood almost knee-high. In the twilight just after sunset, robins and sparrows sang and the first frogs croaked in the swamp. Soon the spring flowers would be appearing.

Judy had been down at the old wharf, trying her luck at fishing. Uncle Walter had said that morning that with spring here the cunners would be coming in. It hadn't been much fun fishing, though. She had missed David bitterly and she hadn't got a single bite. Now there were still the hens to feed before supper. Judy felt tired and cross; she should have caught at least one fish.

"Where have you been all this time, Judy?" Aunt Kate called from the kitchen door.

"Fishing. Uncle Walter was wrong. I didn't catch a single fish."

"David and his father have been here after your uncle," Aunt Kate said. "They're going to burn the big field tonight. They've all gone off together. It's a shame you weren't here to go with them."

"Is it all done?" Judy cried.

"Heavens no. I should think it would take hours to burn that field."

"Then I'll go," Judy said. "I've still got time."

"But your supper!"

"You fix me a sandwich, Aunt Kate, while I feed Sonny Boy." Judy was off to the barn be-

[23]

fore her aunt could say any more. She caught
up the measure and scooped up the grain. On
a gallop she raced to the henhouse door and
threw the grain inside. The big yellow rooster,
Sonny Boy, crackled with rage, and Judy said,
"You'd better keep still. You're lucky to get
any supper tonight." She ran back to the barn
again with the measure, and then, puffing for
breath, to the house.

"Don't hurry so," Aunt Kate said. "There's time enough, but I'm not sure you should go through the wood alone at night. It'll be dark before you get there."

"I know the way; I've been there dozens of times," Judy protested. "But why did they decide to burn the big field? They never did it before." The land behind David's house was called the big field. It had not been used for many years. Once it had been a pasture, but now some of it had gone back into blueberry land.

"David's father has bought a cow," Aunt Kate said. "He's going to use part of the big field as a pasture, and he wants to get rid of the old grass so that there will be some nice new grass for the cow to eat."

"Will it be a very big fire?" Judy asked.

"I should think it might," Aunt Kate said. "I've nothing to put in this sandwich, Judy, but cheese."

"That's all right," Judy said. "Only be quick. I might miss all the fun."

A few minutes later, dressed in jacket and cap and clutching two slices of bread and a slice of cheese, Judy was ready to go.

"Now you stay on the road, Judy," her aunt warned. "Don't go cutting across fields. And when you get to the big field, keep away from the fire. Find your Uncle Walter first and do what he says."

Judy went along at a dogtrot, chewing bites of the bread and cheese between breaths. The spring twilight was brief. Already the road was hidden in shadow. I *would* have to miss something good, she thought. The first really exciting thing in ages happens and I have to be off fishing. She swallowed the last of the bread and cheese and pulled the collar of her jacket about her face. The April night was raw and cold.

The last robin had stopped singing, but from

the swamp beside the road the clamor of the frogs was almost deafening. The road led under the thick branches of some giant spruces, becoming almost spooky. Judy was not really afraid, she knew that there was nothing on Cape Oregon that could hurt her, but she did wish that Uncle Walter or David were with her, just for company. From an old brush-grown field a nighthawk called; it did not sound like a bird but rather like some hobgoblin.

Now in the darkness it seemed to Judy that she heard footsteps coming along the road behind her. It was only the echo of her own steps, that she knew, but she wished she had remembered to take Aunt Kate's flashlight. A light would be very comforting just now. Suddenly she changed the trot to a run, noticing that the steps behind her began running too. She was coming out of the woods, it was not so dark here, and she could even see the sky. The road was rising to the top of a high hill, and for the first time she had a good chance to look ahead of her.

Judy stopped and caught her breath. She looked north, and then she forgot all about nighthawks or footsteps or hobgoblins. The whole world seemed to be on fire. To the north was a vast, unearthly glow, which the overcast sky reflected. Although no flames showed, the sky looked like some giant glowing pit or oven.

Her first fear was that the fire would be all over before she got there. Then the dreadful thought came, supposing the fire had got away from them, supposing all Cape Oregon should burn up? She began to run faster than when the ghostly footsteps had followed her.

The fire was a long way from being over, Judy discovered when she got there. Nor was there any danger of its getting out of control. Like so many things at night, fire often looks worse than it is. When she reached the edge of the big field the fire came down to meet her,

[28]

running in a little ripple only a few inches high, over the dead grass and leaves and into the ditch beside the road. Mr. Young was standing there armed with an old broom, watching to see that the flames did not get into the woods.

"Well, Judy, where did you come from?" he asked, looking in the flickering firelight like some witch with a broomstick.

Judy gasped for breath. "Coming along the road, it looked as if the whole world was on fire."

"Like enough it does," Mr. Young agreed. "Over to Summerport they'll say the Cape is burning up."

"Can't I help?" Judy asked, when she had caught her breath.

"There's nothing to do here," Mr. Young said. "It'll burn itself out in the ditch. Why don't you go up where David is? Maybe you can be of some help there."

Judy saw that a car was parked on the road

ahead. Shadowy figures moved around its headlights, and voices called. Judy ran on to the car and, remembering her aunt's warning, she called her uncle's name. Uncle Walter did not answer and Judy saw that she stood now in the dead center of the burning. On every side the black, newly burned field spread out before her, but the lower end of the field was just beginning to burn, the fire rippling away from her into the night.

There were people around her, but in the uncertain light of the fire it was hard to tell who they were. Judy called to her uncle again, and then someone told her that he was down where they were setting the fire. Judy started off across the freshly burned field. Beyond the range of the car's headlight it was pitch-dark, and Judy stumbled into an old barbed-wire fence she hadn't even known was there. She caught her jacket on the barbs before she found a hole in the wire and crawled through.

Uncle Walter and David were moving along the bottom of the field, next to the woods. David was setting the fire and Uncle Walter, following him with a portable knapsack sprayer on his shoulder, was putting out any flames that started for the woods.

"I got here at last," Judy said, ignoring David.

Uncle Walter shifted the sprayer onto his other shoulder and said, "Might as well let her set the fire, Dave."

Judy saw that David gathered a handful of dry grass and lighted it from the fire; then he walked along quickly, setting fires with this little torch until the flames nipped his fingers and he had to drop it for a new one. Now he picked up an old piece of brush and dropped in behind Uncle Walter. Judy began setting fire in his place, never noticing when she grabbed a handful of rose briers along with the grass. Behind her Uncle Walter came with the sprayer and put out the fire on the side facing the woods. The flames were only allowed to run in the other direction, into the field. Last of all came David with the brush, putting out any fragment of fire that might have escaped the sprayer and be sneaking back into the woods.

The night seemed very peaceful and lovely with just the three of them in the circle of light. The fire made enough warmth to keep out the night's chill. Judy felt she could do this forever and never grow tired.

"I see Jeb has started work on the old Fuller cottage," David said suddenly, beating out a stubborn bit of flame.

"Yes," Uncle Walter said, "I hear they're going to rent it this summer."

The Fuller cottage was a big house only a mile or so down the road from where Judy lived. It had once been a fine place and it had a lovely view of the bay, but no one had lived in it for many years. Now it was shabby and

run-down, as houses get when they aren't lived in. It needed painting and little trees were sprouting on the lawn.

"It hasn't been rented for years and years," David said. "Leastwise, I can't remember anyone being there."

"It's been a long time," Uncle Walter agreed. "It'll need a lot of work done on it. Let's catch our breath, Judy." They stood and watched the fire. It was converging from all sides on the center of the field. As the wind caught it, it ran faster than a man through the dry grass, rose briers, and old goldenrod stalks. The heat was thrown back against their faces and the field was bright as day.

Judy was thinking, If people live in the Fuller cottage they will go by our house every day. A sudden thought came to her. "Are there any children?" she asked.

"Where?" Uncle Walter had forgotten what they had been talking about.

"The people who are going to live in the Fuller cottage. Have they got any children?"

"Why, I don't know," her uncle said, and added, "Seems like Jeb said there was one."

"How old?" Judy asked.

"I don't really know. Why don't you ask Jeb sometime? Probably he'd know."

They had gone back to setting fire again, but now the ground was wet and swampy, and cold water soaked into Judy's sneakers. David and Uncle Walter had on rubber boots, but Judy had not thought to put on rubbers.

"You go back to the car before your feet get wet," her uncle said. "We're going to be done here in a few minutes. Then we'll go home and your Aunt Kate'll have a hot supper for us."

Judy didn't mind going back; she was tired and hungry and the fire was almost over anyway. She walked across the field toward the distant headlights of the car. All around her was the burned-earth smell of soot and cinders.

Away from the fire it was pitch-black and she would never have been able to find the road if she had not seen the car's lights. Here and there, in the inky darkness, a fence post still glowed, an eerie spot of light.

Judy was weary and her jacket smelled of grass smoke, but her mind was peaceful and happy. She would talk to Jeb soon and find out about the people who were coming to the cottage. In her mind, however, she felt she already knew his answers. There would be a child, a little girl her own age, someone to play with this summer. David's grumpy indifference would no longer matter to her when this new playmate came.

CHAPTER 3

The Bargain

It was a lovely morning early in May. The grass was silky under the hot sun, violets made great purple patches on the meadow, and the ledges were white with strawberry blossoms.

Judy noticed all of these things as she ran across the fields toward the Fuller cottage. By June there would be plenty of wild strawberries to gather. On her way home this afternoon she would stop and pick a bunch of blue violets for Aunt Kate.

Even out here in the fields she could hear the pounding of a hammer at the cottage. Jeb had been working there every pleasant day this month. She caught a glimpse of his blue shirt through the bushes that surrounded the cottage. He was busy on the south porch, where the shaky steps needed new risers. Judy had a very special reason for this visit. No one had been able to tell her much about the family who would spend the summer here, so she had decided to ask Jeb himself. He would surely know.

Judy strolled casually across the lawn as if she were hunting wild flowers instead of having a particular errand in mind. When she saw Jeb glance up, she called to him, "Hi there!"

"Hi, Judy." Jeb was an old man, much older than Uncle Walter. His hair was very white and his face wrinkled, but he was quick and active just the same. Judy had heard her uncle say that Jeb could do more work in a day than most young men. Now he kept right on pounding nails and did not look up again. There was a good smell of newly cut lumber around, and the repaired steps looked bright beside the weathered gray of the porch flooring.

Judy climbed up on the porch and perched on the railing. The cottage, which had looked empty and abandoned ever since she could remember, was beginning to come to life. The shutters were off the windows and the lawn had just been mowed, although it was still rough and shaggy as a lawn will be when it has been neglected for a long time. Judy wondered what the inside of the cottage looked like, but she did not dare ask if she might go inside. Instead, she curled her toes around the posts of the railing and looked downhill at the little blue cove that showed just below the blossoming apple trees. "You've got a lot of work to do," she said at last.

"I'll say I have." Jeb slammed his ruler down on a board, marked it, and then reached for the saw. "They let a place go for ten years and then expect you to have it shipshape overnight."

"When are they coming?" Judy asked.

"First or middle of June. When the kid gets out of school."

Judy's voice remained calm. "Do they have a boy or a girl?"

"Oh, it's a girl, name of Laurel. Round your age, I'd say. Ten or maybe eleven."

Judy kept on curling her toes about the post. She gave no sign that Jeb had told her all she wanted to know in one swoop. "How many of them are there?" she asked calmly.

"Oh, the father and mother and this kid, and a woman to do the housework and cooking. They don't seem to be bad folks, but you know how summer people are, expect everything done in a minute. It's hard to get an old, run-down place like this decent in a short time, and I can't get anyone to help me."

"Why did they ever decide to come to Cape Oregon?" Judy asked.

"Oh, it's one of those things. They wanted to be on the Maine coast this summer, and one of their cousins knew someone who was related to the Fullers. They're going to live very simple, they say. Then it's fix the porch, nail those shingles back on, mow the lawn, paint the window sashes, clean the cottage, get the water and light turned on. Nothing to it, you know."

"I guess you do have a lot of work," Judy agreed. She knew that Jeb wasn't as angry as he sounded, that actually he was pleased with the work, but it was best to agree with him. "I guess I'll be getting home now," she added, dropping from the porch railing to the ground.

Once she was out of Jeb's sight, Judy turned a handspring in the grass. It was going to work out after all. There would be a little girl, just her own age, and there would be no one else for her to play with. Laurel—it was a lovely name. Judy said to herself, tasting the sweetness of the words, "I have a friend named Laurel."

David could lobster on the *North Wind* if he wanted to; she would not need him now. She would show Laurel all the things David had shown her. She would teach her to fish, to dig clams, pick berries, and gather shells. A city girl would not know any more about the shore than Judy had known herself when she had first come to live at her Uncle Walter's.

There was still something to be done. If she had a boat they could roam all along the shore. Uncle Walter's old skiff was too heavy for them to handle alone, but there was the *Pant.* The *Pant* was just large enough for them, and if they had it this summer things would be almost perfect. Instead of taking the path home, Judy turned toward the Youngs' house.

David's mother was hanging the wash out on the line. She was a big stout woman with flashing black eyes. She knew nothing of the quarrel between Judy and David, for the children had kept it to themselves, so now she called out a friendly greeting. "Come on in, Judy, and have a piece of cake."

Judy was glad to accept the offer; she had a little empty spot in her stomach. There was no sign of either David or Mr. Young around the place. Judy thanked Mrs. Young for the piece of chocolate cake; then, perched on the edge of her chair, she asked, "Where's David?"

"Where he spends every spare minute now," his mother answered. "Aboard the *North Wind*. David and his father spend more time aboard that boat then they do at home."

"It's a very nice boat," Judy said politely.

"Yes, it's good as boats go." Mrs. Young was beaming proudly. "It cost a lot of money, but

David thinks as much of it as his Dad does. He's got his heart set on lobstering in it this summer. It'll be hard on you, Judy," she added as an afterthought, "not to have anyone to play with this summer."

Judy wanted to say, "But I will have someone," but she held her tongue. No point in telling her plans too soon. She only said mildly, "I guess I'll go down and look at the *North Wind*. I can see it from the wharf."

"David will take you aboard when he's got time," Mrs. Young said.

"Thank you for the cake," Judy said again, and then ran down the path toward the wharf. A robin flew up from under her feet, a wisp of grass in its beak. It was building a nest nearby.

Before she reached the wharf, Judy passed the *Pant* turned upside down on the banking. She stopped to look at it. Bits of paint were flaking off, and the little boat looked shabby and forlorn. Judy lifted the bow of the punt

and peeked under it. The smell of lobster bait and old dry crabs still lingered there. Judy flaked a bit of paint off with her thumbnail. No, it wasn't going to do the *Pant* a bit of good to lie there all summer.

From the wharf she could see the *North Wind* at its mooring. It *was* a beautiful boat, Judy had to be honest and admit it, and it did make Uncle Walter's boat, which was moored beside it, look small and dumpy. The *North*

Wind had a high, proud bow. The boat had been newly painted white with green trimmings.

Judy was leaning against the wharf railing when she heard footsteps on the loose planks behind her. David was coming down the wharf carrying a jug of water.

"Hi there," Judy said.

"Hello." David was a little uncertain. It was clear that he hadn't forgotten the quarrel and wasn't sure they were on speaking terms. But Judy had more important things than a quarrel to think of now.

"You've got a lovely boat," she said admiringly. "Did you and your dad do the painting?"

"Yep," David said. He put the jug of water into a skiff that was tied to the landing float. "I think green looks better than yellow. That's the trimming she had before."

"It's too bad you won't have time to paint the *Pant*," Judy went on. "Uncle Walter says it isn't good for a boat to lie around in the weather without being painted."

"Oh, I might get the time," David said lightly.

"If *I* painted her and furnished the paint myself," she said quickly, "could I use her this summer?"

David stared at her. "I thought you got mad when we talked about her before."

"I just want her to play around in," Judy said. "I'm not going lobstering, so I can't pay money for her. But if I painted her and used her, she'd be better off than if she were lying on the banking."

David felt that he should get something for the use of his punt, but he knew, too, that Judy was right. It was bad for the *Pant* to lie on the banking all summer without paint or care. If he didn't have to buy paint or bother with the painting, something would be gained, and the *Pant* would be better off for it. And David's conscience bothered him a little over the mean things he had said to Judy.

So he said grudgingly, "All right, since it's you. But I wouldn't let anyone else have her like that—for nothing, I mean. And you be sure to do a good job on the painting, and mind that you always keep her tied and don't let anything happen to her."

"Oh, I'll be careful," Judy promised.

"Tell you what," David said, growing more friendly. "I've got to take this water out to Dad. Why don't you come with me and see the *North Wind?* She's swell, a real cabin, bunks, everything."

CHAPTER 4

The Catboat

Now that it was June, the brief summer at
Cape Oregon was stepping into high gear.
There was more work than anyone could pos-
sibly do, though there were more hours of daylight. Old Jeb was not the only one to com-
plain now. But Jeb had worked faithfully, and
the Fuller cottage had changed from the seedy,
run-down place of a month ago into a cottage
bright with paint and fitted with a new porch.
The lawn, however, still looked a little raw
where it had been freshly cut.

David and his father had loaded the *Pant* onto their truck and brought it over to Uncle Walter's. "If you're going to have her you might as well have her," Mr. Young had said. "No need to tramp way over to our place every time you want to slap a little paint on her."

Judy had promptly gone to work on her uncle to wheedle from him the leftover paint up in the barn loft. "You won't use it, Uncle Walter, and it'll only harden up if it stays there."

"You don't say!" Uncle Walter said, his eyes twinkling. "You wouldn't have had that paint in mind when you bargained for the *Pant,* now would you?"

"Well, yes," Judy confessed. "I couldn't pay any money for her and I just had to have her."

"I should think it would be lonely for you, fooling around in her without David."

Judy gave him a thoughtful glance, then decided to risk telling. "You know those people who are coming to the Fuller cottage this summer? Well, I asked Jeb about them and they have a little girl just my age."

"Yes?" Uncle Walter didn't seem able to put two and two together.

"Don't you see?" Judy said impatiently. "There isn't anyone for *her* to play with either. I bet she'll be lonely too."

"You think she will want to play with you, and that is why you want the *Pant*," Uncle Walter said.

"Well, I sort of hoped it would work out like that."

"Judy, there are all kinds of little girls in this world, you must know that." Uncle Walter stopped abruptly, and then went on. "If her family planned on coming here this summer, they must have known it would be lonely for the child. Probably they have plans of their own. They may be bringing friends with them."

"No," Judy said. "I asked Jeb and he said

just the little girl and her parents and someone to do the cooking."

"You seem to know all about it. But perhaps she won't want to play with you, or you with her."

"You're just trying to be gloomy," Judy said. "Anyway, I can hope."

"This isn't getting the *Pant* fixed," Uncle Walter said. "We'd better get that paint."

They walked to the barn together. Her uncle was so good, Judy thought. She had known he wouldn't refuse her the paint. It wouldn't really have spoiled if it hadn't been used, and it was kind of him to let her have it.

Suddenly they heard a car coming along the road and they both stopped to look. A car was something unusual on this road. It might be David and his father, but the motor didn't make as much noise as the Youngs' old car.

A big yellow truck moved slowly up the road,

feeling its way cautiously over the bumps and the potholes. The driver was a stranger, but there was no mistaking his companion, who waved to them cheerily. It was Jeb. But neither Judy nor Uncle Walter even noticed Jeb, for they were staring at the trailer that was being towed behind the truck. It was a modern, steel boat trailer, painted a bright red, and on it rested the sweetest little red-and-white sailboat that Judy had ever laid eyes on. Even dismantled, with its mast down, it looked saucy and bright.

The truck disappeared around a bend in the road, heading for the Fuller cottage, but Judy and her uncle continued to stare after it. Then Judy said slowly, "A real sailboat."

"Yep," Uncle Walter said. "Prettiest little catboat I've seen in a long time."

Judy thought of the *Pant* lying there in the dooryard. It was awfully small and shabby and unimportant compared with a sailboat.

Even when she was painted, the *Pant* couldn't compete with that.

Her uncle looked down into Judy's troubled face. He seemed to know what was wrong. "I wouldn't worry over it, Judy," he said. "Likely enough it belongs to her pa or someone else in the family."

"Even so," Judy said, "who'd want a punt when they had a real sailboat?"

"It's no help to be disappointed," Uncle Walter said. "If a punt is all you've got, you'll have to make the best of it. You might not have been too happy with the girl, anyway. Now let's have a look at that paint."

It was not until suppertime that Judy remembered his words. She had come into the kitchen covered with paint. "Good heavens, Judy!" Aunt Kate said. "Did you paint the boat or yourself? Get some kerosene and wash that paint off; then try some hot water and soap."

"She does look swell," Judy said, almost

happy again. "You know, I'd rather have the *Pant* than a catboat after all."

"What are you talking about?" Aunt Kate asked.

"I thought maybe the little girl who's coming here this summer might want to come rowing with me, but she's already got a boat."

"What little girl?" Aunt Kate asked.

"The people who rented the Fuller cottage, they have a little girl."

"Oh, summer people." There was a change in Aunt Kate's voice. Judy heard it, but she could not tell what it meant. Disapproval? Uncertainty?

"Why do you call them summer people?" Judy said.

"Because they are here only in the summer."

"Oh, I know that. I mean, why do you say it that way, as if there was something wrong with them?"

"I don't even know them," Aunt Kate said shortly.

"Uncle Walter said something too, while we were getting the paint for the *Pant*," Judy said thoughtfully. "Something about the girl not wanting to play with me. What did he mean?"

"Well." Aunt Kate put out the soap, the hot water, and the jug of kerosene. "It's hard to explain, Judy. The people who come here in the summer spend most of their time in a city or in another part of the country. They have a different life from ours. They have different likes and dislikes, different problems, and different ways of settling them. We don't understand them very well, and they don't understand us. Your uncle meant that the girl at the Fuller cottage might not want to play with you, because she may think you aren't interesting enough. Or she may play with you for a while and then drop you as soon as she gets tired of you. And she'll have a lot of things, Judy, that you won't have. I don't want you to become envious or jealous."

"She's got a catboat, I know that already," Judy said. "But I don't mind."

"Her parents will have a great many other things that your uncle and I can't afford."

"I know that," Judy said. "But I can't see how it will make any difference. But probably she won't want to play with me if she has a boat of her own," she added quickly, because she thought it might comfort her aunt.

Outside the kitchen door Judy rubbed the kerosene over her paint-stained fingers and then let it trickle to the ground. She wouldn't let the catboat trouble her, or her aunt's worries either. She had gone too far to retreat now. The *Pant* was hers for a whole summer, and she would follow Uncle Walter's advice and make the best of it.

CHAPTER 5

Laurel

Judy was on an errand for her aunt. Now that it was summer, Uncle Walter didn't bother to come home for dinner but worked all day long with his traps. He wouldn't take a lunch with him, but every noon Aunt Kate sent Judy, with a package of sandwiches and a Thermos of coffee, down to the old wharf. If her uncle wasn't working there, Judy took the *Pant* and rowed out to the lobster car. She would always find Uncle Walter there and give him his dinner.

June had been almost a perfect month; the long bright days were not marred by even a shower. Aunt Kate complained that the lettuce was drying up and Uncle Walter shook his head over the yellowing hayfield, but Judy hoped that the sunshine would never end.

Now she trudged along, Uncle Walter's lunch in one hand and the Thermos bottle under the other arm. The wharf was deserted; all the boats were out pulling traps in the perfect weather. Only the little *Pant* was there, tied to the old float. Judy put her bundles down and pulled the punt in beside the float. The *North Wind's* mooring lay empty too; Judy almost never saw David, now that school was out.

The gray worn planks of the wharf were actually hot to touch. The sun, reflected on the still water, made a glare that hurt the eyes. Even the gulls seemed to be trying to escape the heat; there was not a bird in the cove.

Uncle Walter must be out at the lobster car,

Judy thought, and she would have to take his dinner out to him. The *Pant* looked bright and cheerful in its new coat of paint, but even it seemed half asleep, nosing its reflection in the sea. The *Pant* was a darling, Judy thought, even if things had not turned out the way she had hoped. The family in the Fuller cottage had been here a week now and Judy had not laid eyes on one of them.

Uncle Walter's lobster car, the big crate in which he kept his lobsters alive until he could sell them, was moored in the next cove. Judy steadied the *Pant* with one hand while she put the sandwiches and the Thermos aboard. Then she stepped in herself, feeling the *Pant* come to life beneath her. She untied the boat, slipped the oars into place, and began rowing. Once her fingers dipped into the water, and she found it was icy cold to touch. But in the sunny cove the very shore seemed to dance with the heat.

As soon as she rounded the point she saw that her uncle's old green powerboat was lying beside the lobster car. The car was really just a big box weighted down enough to keep its top level with the surface of the water. The sea flowed through it and kept the lobsters cool and lively. There was a door in the top of the car that could be opened so that the lobsters could be dipped out. Her uncle had come in from pulling his traps and had stopped to put the lobsters he had caught into the car. Then, finding a plank loose, he had decided to repair it.

He looked up as Judy pulled up on the other side of the car. "Here you are again," he said. "Kate might have saved you the trouble of coming out in this heat. I'll be home as soon as I fix this plank."

"You always say that, but you never come," Judy said, handing over the lunch. "Did you catch many lobsters?"

"Not bad." Uncle Walter always said the same thing, even when there was hardly a lobster in the traps. "Want a cooky, Judy?"

"I've just had my dinner," Judy answered.

"Well, it's a good thing you came along after all," her uncle said. "I saved a bucket of crabs for you and I came near forgetting them." He lifted a pail filled with greenish-brown crabs into the *Pant*. "You take them home and boil them, and we'll have them cold for supper. I could eat a dozen of them right now."

Crab meat was a treat, and it had been a long time since Uncle Walter had caught any crabs as fine as these. Still, Aunt Kate would have to build up a new fire to cook them, for she always let the wood fire go out on a hot afternoon like this.

"You had better get some damp rockweed, Judy, and pack it over those crabs," her uncle warned. "They're blowing bubbles now and they won't live long in this heat."

Judy rowed in to the nearby sand beach. She stepped out as soon as the *Pant* grounded in shoal water. The sneakers that she wore were so old and battered that they were not good for much except to protect her feet from the sharp shells and stones. So it didn't really matter if they were wet or dry. The water felt wonderfully cool and good after the hot sun. The ledges were covered with rockweed, which floated out in the tide like coarse brown hair. Between the patches of rockweed the sandy bottom was sprinkled with white clamshells.

Judy pulled an armful of the tough weed, feeling the salt water soak through her shirt and her old dungarees. It felt good and cold, although it certainly was messy. She dumped the rockweed into the *Pant*, then stood a moment to catch her breath. For some reason she glanced toward the shore and found herself looking straight into the eyes of another little girl. She was sitting on a point of ledge that jutted out into the cove, and for a second the two children stared at one another without speaking. Then a flood of embarrassment and anger swept over Judy. She was conscious of her stringy hair and her dripping shirt. The other girl must have been there all the time, watching her; she could at least have spoken. It was almost like being spied upon, Judy thought.

As if she read Judy's thought, a half-smile passed over the stranger's face. She rose gracefully and stepped down into the water. She looked as if she was around Judy's age and she was dressed much like Judy, in battered sneakers and faded blue dungarees. Yet there was a difference. Perhaps it was the smooth, even tan that covered her arms and legs, instead of the patchy, half-red sunburn that Judy had. Perhaps it was the easy way in which she moved.

The new girl waded out and rested a hand

[70]

on the *Pant's* bow. "My name is Laurel," she said. "What's yours?"

Judy had known from the first moment who she was; there wasn't any other strange girl at Cape Oregon. But even if she hadn't known she would have somehow guessed, for the name Laurel fitted her so well. Her hair was bright in the sun, her eyes were gray, and there was the faintest dusting of freckles over the turned-up nose.

Judy gave her name and then said crossly, "Why didn't you yell or something? I didn't see you."

"I know you didn't." There was that quick, impish smile again. Then Laurel's mood changed, and she became eager to please. "I know how you feel. I hate to be watched when I don't know about it. It's like being spied on. But you were having such a good time and I was wondering what you wanted the rockweed for."

There was no resisting that grin, and Judy smiled. "I guess you scared me more than anything. I had to get rockweed to put over these crabs."

Laurel peeped into the bucket. "They're going to die if you don't do something with them pretty quickly."

"I know," Judy said. "I've got to get them home. Aunt Kate will have to build up a fire and cook them even if it is awfully hot."

Laurel reached her hand into the bucket and took out a crab. Judy noticed, with surprise and approval, that she handled it just as one should handle a crab, placing her fingers on the top of the shell, where the claws could not reach them.

"Why don't you bring them over to my house and cook them?" Laurel asked.

"Oh, no!" Judy said, quite shocked. She thought of her wet dungarees and her dirty sneakers. Aunt Kate would be horrified if she knew that Judy had gone into a stranger's house dressed like this.

"Oh, my folks are out, cook and all," Laurel said lightly, as if she knew just what was wrong. "So you needn't be scared."

"I'm not scared," Judy said coldly. Laurel had a way of guessing her thoughts that was too close for comfort. "It's just that my aunt wouldn't want her cooking done in someone else's house."

"But we have an electric stove. You turn the switch and it's on. It isn't any trouble on a hot day."

"Well, I can't do it," Judy said stubbornly.

"But your aunt would be ever so pleased if you took them home all cooked and she didn't have to bother with them. She's probably tired and it's hot; this would save her so much work." Laurel looked up with her sweetest smile. "We could row around to my beach; it's not very far. I'd love to row, would you let me?"

"Well, yes," Judy said gruffly. She did not really know how to stand up against Laurel's coaxing.

Laurel pushed the *Pant* free and stepped into it so easily that the punt did not even rock. She knew about boats, all right. "You've got a very fine boat," she said.

Judy looked at her quickly, but the brown face was perfectly sober. "It's only a punt," Judy said. "You have a real catboat, haven't you?"

"Yes. The *Cheshire* is nice, but I think a punt is even nicer. A sailboat can be tippy, you know, and it's lots more fun to get in close to shore, don't you think so?"

Judy was a little dazed, for she had never thought of having a choice between a catboat and a punt. But now Laurel, who could have either, said that she preferred the punt. Judy smiled and almost told her why she had gotten the *Pant* this summer, but some inner warning caused her to hold her tongue. As yet, she didn't know Laurel very well.

Laurel chattered on easily, not seeming to notice Judy's silence. She talked of what they had been doing, how they had gone fishing every day but had not caught anything but sculpins. Before she realized it, Judy was telling her where the best spot for flounders was located.

Just as they turned into Laurel's cove the *North Wind* passed them, running in to her mooring. Judy had a moment of panic when she thought of what David would say when he saw a stranger rowing the *Pant*. Laurel feathered her oars, easing the *Pant* against the swell caused by the bigger boat; then she turned and said, "That's the boat that has a boy who looks like a sculpin aboard."

"What?" Judy said in astonishment.

Laurel gave her a sharp look. "I hope he isn't a friend of yours, but he looks just like a sculpin. You know how they have a big fin running down their back? Well, his hair stands up like a fin and he's sort of popeyed, and goodness knows he's got as many spines as a sculpin. I asked him if I could go out with them some day when they pulled their traps, and he popped out his eyes and stuck out all his spines and said they never took 'summer people out in their boat.' " Her last words were a mimicry of David's tone.

Judy giggled in spite of herself. David did look a little bit like a sculpin, with his unruly, too long hair. She could understand, too, his horror of having any one like Laurel aboard the *North Wind.* Of course, it was wrong for Laurel to make fun of him, but . . . . "I do know him," Judy said slowly.

Laurel gazed calmly at the shore, picking a good spot to land. "Well, when you see him, tell him I've seen plenty of boats just as good as that tub he calls the *North Wind.*"

[78]

Judy was shocked once more. The *North Wind* was a very fine boat, the best at Cape Oregon. How could Laurel speak that way about it? Had she really seen boats just as good?

CHAPTER 6

At Laurel's House

Earlier in the summer, when Judy had visited the Fuller cottage to talk with Jeb, she had not gone beyond the porch. Now, as she tramped across the lawn, she was filled with curiosity, but she was apprehensive, too. What would Aunt Kate ever say if she knew that Judy was going into a strange house, shabby and dirty as she was now? "Are you sure your folks aren't at home?" she asked again.

"Sure. Positive. Give you my word," Laurel

said gaily. "I bet your aunt would give you Hail Columbia if she knew you were coming in here dressed like that!"

Judy set the bucket of crabs down and stood staring at the other girl. "How did you know —that?" she finished lamely. What she wanted to say was, "How do you know everything I'm thinking?" But she could not get the words out.

"I've seen people like your aunt before. I know what they think." But then Laurel veered away from the subject. "You don't look any worse than I do," she said mildly. "Leave the crabs here by the kitchen door. I'll show you the place first." Everyone called the place a cottage, but there were more rooms in it than there were in Judy's house. Laurel darted back and forth, opening doors and giving Judy a quick glimpse of the many rooms. Judy felt lost; she couldn't even remember what part of the house she was in. There were polished floors that gleamed under heavy, dark-colored rugs. There were odd-looking pictures on the walls, and at least a half-dozen fireplaces. The rooms were cool even on this hot day, but they had an unlived-in look; even the fireplaces looked too spotless to have ever seen a fire.

"It must be nice to live here," Judy said, because she didn't want to hurt Laurel's feelings.

"It's not so much," Laurel said. "What I mean is, it's just rented, it's not our own." She led the way back to the kitchen. "It's like being a turtle and living in a borrowed shell. You have your own shell, because your home belongs to you. When are you going to show me your house?"

Judy felt a hard lump in her stomach. What would her aunt say if she should bring Laurel home with her? For the first time, it came to her mind that the old farmhouse was rather small and shabby and it did need painting.

When she had been with David this had never entered her mind. Her house was just as good as David Young's house. To get away from a dangerous subject she asked, "Do you just rent houses wherever you go?"

"Oh, no, we own a house, too. But it's in Florida. Do you know where that is?"

"Of course," Judy said coldly. "I study geography in school."

"It's right on the Gulf," Laurel went on dreamily. "You could throw a rock from the porch into the water. We go swimming and sailing all the time. The water is so clear that you can look way down and see the coral and the little fish swimming over it. Have you ever seen live coral?"

"No," Judy said shortly.

Laurel was pulling out a kettle to put the crabs in. "If only it wasn't so hot in summer I'd like to stay there all the year."

After Laurel had dumped the crabs into the

boiling water, Judy looked around the kitchen. It was as large as the other rooms; its white walls looked as if they had been sliced out of a cake of ice. There was a huge white sink, a huge white electric stove, a huge white re-frigerator. The little kitchen in Uncle Walter's house would be lost in here.

Laurel was perched on a tall white kitchen stool. "Now you can tell me about this David," she said.

"There isn't anything to tell."

"I suppose you've known him all your life."

"I've known him as long as I've been at Cape Oregon," Judy corrected. Laurel was silent and at length Judy went on. "His name is David Young. He's a year older than I am and he lives in that house down in the cove. Last summer I helped him set lobster pots and we went clam-ming and fishing together."

"And this summer you don't do any of those

things." Laurel touched the tender spot un-
erringly.

"Well, no." Judy's voice was unhappy.

"Did you have a fight, or does he just think
he doesn't want to be bothered with girls?"

How can a friend be explained to a stranger?
For David was a friend, even if he had been
unfair to her, even if she had quarreled with
him. "Oh, David's all right," Judy said shortly.
And then to keep Laurel from asking more un-
pleasant questions she asked, "Have you really
seen better boats than the *North Wind*?"

"Sure I have. We—I mean—someone I know
in Florida owns a boat that would make David's
eyes stick out."

"But the *North Wind* must be pretty good,"
Judy insisted. "My Uncle Walter says she's the
best boat he's ever seen."

Laurel would not argue with her. "It's not
bad for a fishing boat. I'd like to go out in her.

David was just plain mean when he refused to take me."

"Perhaps Uncle Walter would take you sometime," Judy offered. But she could not help thinking that if Laurel had not thought highly of the *North Wind* she would surely think that Uncle Walter's shabby little boat wasn't any better than a shingle.

"Maybe." Laurel showed little interest in the offer. Her mind was off on something else. "Do you know, it would be fun to play a trick on David! Pay him back for being so mean to us, and show him he isn't so much after all."

"What could we do?" Judy asked in wonderment. The idea had never entered her head of paying David back for his meanness.

"We might do something to the *North Wind*," Laurel suggested.

"Oh, no!" Judy was truly shocked. "You can't touch someone's boat. Not when he's using it to work with."

"Oh, forget it," Laurel said quickly. "I didn't mean it. I just said it for a joke." Just at this moment the kettle of crabs boiled over and a shower of steam rose up in the air. Both girls scrambled for the kettle; they had forgotten all about the crabs. Laurel peeped into the grillwork over the electric coil; her face was anxious. "I hope nothing got inside the stove," she said.

"Would you like to have some?" Judy asked.

"I can't take your aunt's crabs."

"But we cooked them here. She wouldn't mind. We can get more any time. Please take some."

"No," Laurel said firmly. "But tell you what"—she turned to Judy with a friendly smile —"maybe I can come over to your house some-day and we can take your little boat and go for a picnic or something."

"I don't know," Judy said, without any an-swering smile. "Aunt Kate worries when I go out in the boat." Actually Judy was still uneasy over that remark about the *North Wind*. Even though Laurel had quickly denied that she was serious, the thought remained with Judy—would she really damage someone's boat just to get even with him?

CHAPTER 7

Cow's in the Corn

Judy had every intention of asking Aunt Kate if Laurel couldn't come over to play the very next day, but things turned out differently. She had feared that her aunt would be displeased about the crabs, but Aunt Kate was even more unhappy than she expected.

"You mean that you just walked into a stranger's house and used her dishes and cooked on her stove?" her aunt asked, as if she could not believe such a thing was possible.

"Well, Laurel asked me," Judy said.

"Just a child," Aunt Kate said. "What does a child know about cluttering up a kitchen? Where was her mother?"

"Her mother wasn't there," Judy answered. "They have a maid and I bet she washed everything up."

At the mention of a maid, Aunt Kate pursed her lips and looked crosser than ever. "You must never, never do this again, Judy. I will not have you pestering strangers. And dressed the way you were too! They must have thought you had escaped from the poorhouse."

Judy thought, No one saw me but Laurel, and she didn't look any better than I did. But she said nothing, for the whole adventure seemed to have gone wrong, and now it left a bitter taste in her mouth. She would never have gone home with Laurel if she had not thought that she would be saving her aunt the trouble of building a fire on a hot day and cooking the crabs herself. Aunt Kate didn't understand this; all she thought about was that Judy had shown a lack of manners in going into a stranger's house. She wouldn't even praise the crabs or say that they were well cooked.

Judy knew that this was not a wise time to ask her aunt about Laurel's visit. The next day Uncle Walter asked if Judy didn't want to come with him when he pulled his traps. The day after, Aunt Kate said that the blueberries were ripe in the upper pasture and that she needed a lot of berries to can and would pay as much as fifteen cents a quart for them. Judy had never been paid anything for picking blueberries before, so this was a chance she couldn't miss. So Judy was very busy the next few days, the *Pant* stayed on the shore, and Laurel slipped into the background. It never occurred to Judy that perhaps her aunt had planned it this way.

✿   ✿   ✿

Aunt Kate was very seldom away from home, but early this morning, before the heat of the day, she had walked over to Mrs. Young's to ask about her new recipe for blueberry muffins. She would be able to make good use of it, for the house was simply overflowing with blueberries. Judy had been left at home to do the breakfast dishes. Her aunt had not been gone very long when Judy looked out of the window, and there was Bossy, the red cow, right in the middle of the garden. She must have worked her rope loose and got out of the field where she was supposed to be pastured. She was headed now straight for Uncle Walter's sweet-corn patch. Judy wasn't afraid of Bossy as long as the cow was tied, but she wasn't sure she dared take hold of the halter and lead her into the barn all by herself.

At first she thought of running down to the Youngs' and getting Aunt Kate, but it was perfectly plain that there wouldn't be any garden by the time they got back. I shouldn't be afraid, Judy thought. It's only Bossy, and I've fed her plenty of times. Quite resolutely she went out of the house and down to the garden. She had not intended to hurry, for she might frighten the cow, but when she saw Bossy pull off a whole mouthful of cornstalks she began to run.

"There now. That's a good girl." She had heard her uncle use these words when he talked to the cow, and she hoped they sounded familiar to Bossy. The cow turned and looked at her, chewing thoughtfully, a blade of corn sticking out of her mouth. Judy took a firm hold on the leather strap that made up the halter around Bossy's head. It took a lot of courage, for the cow was very big; in fact, she was tall enough to look right over Judy's head.

"Come on, Bossy." Judy pulled gently at first, then with all her strength. The cow paid less attention to her than she would have paid a fly. Her rough pink tongue licked in the blade of corn. Then she turned her head and almost lifted Judy off her feet as she reached for another bite of corn.

Judy was too furious to be afraid. She braced her feet to keep from being pulled along with the cow. Suddenly someone giggled behind her, and there was Laurel, standing on the edge of the garden and bursting with laughter. She must have come up the road and have been watching the whole time. But she could no longer keep quiet when she saw the cow pulling Judy, instead of Judy pulling the cow.

Bossy looked at the stranger with mild surprise. Judy felt angrier than ever, angry at Bossy for refusing to mind and angry at Laurel for her laughter. "Maybe *you* know how to lead a cow," she said bitterly.

Laurel came up, wiping tears of laughter away with her shirt sleeve. "I'm sorry. I didn't mean to laugh, but you looked so funny."

"She should come," Judy said, "but she just won't, and I can't pull her. Do you know anything about a cow?"

"Not a thing," Laurel said cheerfully. But she was not afraid of the cow, and she came up and took hold of the halter too. "Maybe we can outpull her."

But they couldn't. Bossy was stronger than both the girls. She wasn't mean about it; she just turned her head, braced her feet, and kept on crunching corn.

"Does she like carrots?" Laurel asked. "I've read about getting a donkey to move by holding carrots in front of it."

"I don't think she likes them," Judy said. "But she sure likes this corn."

Then Laurel took a firmer hold on the halter with one hand and with the other she reached out and slapped Bossy on the flank. "Come on, cow," she ordered, and Bossy came on. Perhaps she was tired of corn, or perhaps she recognized more authority in Laurel's tone than in Judy's. At any rate, she allowed them to lead her into the barn.

"I'll put her in the stall," Judy said. "She's broken the rope in the pasture and I'll never get it tied right."

Laurel was waiting at the barn door. For the first time Judy realized that she had company; she had been too busy worrying over the cow to think of it before. She tried to remember her manners. "Aunt Kate isn't home, but please come into the house."

"I thought we would see each other again before this," Laurel said.

"I had to pick berries and there was so much to do." Judy was wondering what Laurel would think of her house. It would look very small compared to the Fuller cottage.

"I knew we might not be allowed to take your boat out, but I waited and waited for you to come to our house again," Laurel said sadly.

"Then Mother said probably you were waiting for an invitation. She said Maine people never went anywhere without being invited."

They were in the kitchen by this time, and Laurel didn't try to hide her curiosity. It was plain that she was just as interested in Judy's house as Judy had been in hers. But to Judy the house had changed. The little kitchen that was always so bright and cheerful now seemed cramped and ugly. The big black wood-burning stove, which was the heart of the house, seemed old-fashioned compared to the shiny white electric stove in Laurel's kitchen. Laurel was looking at the stove now. "Whatever makes it go?" she asked.

Judy lifted a stove cover and explained. "You put some newspaper in first, then some fine wood and bark for kindling, then you light it and keep adding larger pieces of wood."

"Just like a fireplace," Laurel said delightedly. She sat down in a kitchen chair and stuck

the toes of her sneakers between the rungs. "I think you have a lovely house, Judy. I wish our kitchen had bright picture wallpaper like this. I get tired of looking at plain old white walls."

Judy went on washing the last of the dishes. "I like it," she said, and a warm, comforting feeling filled her heart. Laurel thought her home was nice after all. "Aunt Kate will be upset because she was away when you came. But she'll be back pretty soon; she never stays away from home for long."

"What I came for was to tell you there are mackerel in our cove, thousands of them, and I wondered if you could come fishing with me."

"I'll have to ask Aunt Kate first," Judy said doubtfully. "I don't know if she'll let me go."

Laurel glanced out of the window. "Here she comes now. Let me handle it, Judy. I can fix it so she'll say yes."

CHAPTER 8

Mackerel

Aunt Kate was hurrying up the path. Judy threw open the door and called, "Aunt Kate, this is Laurel."

"Who?" Her aunt looked in astonishment at the strange child.

"It's Laurel, the girl who lives over at the Fuller cottage." Laurel had jumped out of her chair and now she came and shook hands with Judy's aunt in a most grown-up fashion.

[104]

"How do you do, Mrs. Brown?" she said, and looked up with a charming smile.

"I'm glad that you can come over and play with Judy," Aunt Kate said, but her face was flushed and she looked around uneasily to see if the kitchen was clean and neat.

"She helped me with the cow," Judy said, eager to put in a good word for Laurel. "Bossy untied her rope and got into the garden, and I couldn't get her out alone."

"What I really came for," Laurel said, smiling, "was to see if Judy could come out in my sailboat this afternoon."

"Sailing?" Aunt Kate's face grew pale. "Oh, dear, I'm afraid not. Not in that little sailboat. It's very kind of you to ask, but I'd rather she didn't go."

Aunt Kate clearly expected an argument, but Judy said nothing and Laurel promptly changed her tactics. "Oh, I'm sorry! But perhaps we could go fishing for mackerel in Judy's punt. *That* would be all right, wouldn't it, Mrs. Brown?"

"Well, yes," Aunt Kate said, caught off guard. After all, she couldn't say no to everything Laurel suggested, and mackerel fishing was much safer, in her mind, than sailing. "Only I'm afraid Judy hasn't any bait."

"Oh, I've got bait and lines and everything," Laurel said smoothly. "All we need is Judy's little boat."

"I can go, can't I?" Judy asked, and there was not much her aunt could say against it.

"Remember, you must be home early," Aunt Kate said. She looked around. "Where are your lines and the bait, Laurel? I didn't notice you had anything with you."

"Oh, they're in a basket out by the fence. I put them down when I saw Judy with the cow."

"My goodness"—Aunt Kate shook her head—

"you're a strange child. What would you have done if I had said no?"

"But I knew that you wouldn't," Laurel said sweetly. "I knew you must be a nice person. Judy says such nice things about you."

Aunt Kate was plainly flattered. She opened the cupboard door and took out two little blueberry cakes and handed one to each girl. "Now be careful in that boat and don't fool around in it or get too far away from the shore."

"Of course we won't," Judy assured her.

"We'll be very careful," Laurel said. "And thank you for the cake."

"You were awfully sure about it," Judy said afterward, when they had picked up the wicker basket and were heading for the shore. "Supposing Aunt Kate *had* said no. Supposing I hadn't wanted to go."

"I knew I could handle your aunt," Laurel said confidently. "Her kind is easy to handle. I bet I can even get her to let you go out in the *Cheshire* after I've had a chance to work on her a few times."

"How about me?" Judy asked. "Am I easy too?"

Laurel grinned. "I knew you'd be just as glad to come as I am to have you."

The *Pant*, which had not been used the whole week, was waiting. Laurel bailed out the little water that was in it and untied it while Judy brought down the oars. "Why did you name her the *Panther Eye?*" Laurel asked.

"I didn't, really," Judy said. "You see, she isn't my boat. She belongs to David, but I have her for the summer."

"Oh," Laurel said, and her eyes grew thoughtful. "Our dear friend, David."

"I didn't know he was your friend," Judy said seriously. "I thought you didn't like him."

"That's just a way of speaking," Laurel said. "Don't let's talk about him. Have you ever fished for mackerel?"

"Yes," Judy said. "Uncle Walter and I have tried it, but they never bit very well."

"Mackerel are funny," Laurel answered. "Sometimes they bite well, but mostly they don't."

They had rowed over to the cove in front of the Fuller cottage by this time. The sun had dropped behind the tops of the trees, so that long, cool shadows spread out over the water. Laurel was rowing and now she rested on her oars. "Look." She pointed, and ahead of her little circles spread out on the still water. They were made by fish that were coming to the surface.

"Fish are breaking," Judy said. "Let's get the lines ready."

In the basket Laurel had two fishlines, some live clams for bait, and a lard can filled with finely chopped clams. This was called throw bait and was used to lure the fish close to the boat. Laurel threw a handful of it overboard and it spread a milky stain over the clear water. Both girls threw their lines over and just then a dark shadow flitted under the punt. The fish struck so hard that Judy nearly tumbled off the seat in surprise. She was used to the steady pull of a flounder or a sculpin and was not prepared for the flashing fight of the mackerel.

"Pull it in! Quick!" Laurel cried, and then she was struggling with her own fish.

The slender blue-green fish came flipping into the boat, where they flapped about wildly. But there was no time to bother with them. The cove seemed full of fish, and as fast as they could get a line out they caught mackerel. Then suddenly the fish were gone.

"Throw some more bait out!" Judy cried. "Keep them coming!"

In a minute the school was back. While the fish were biting it was wildly exciting. Fish were flying in all directions and Judy was busy pulling hers off the hook or dodging the ones

Laurel was flipping into the boat. She did not notice the approaching skiff until it almost bumped into the *Pant.*

David Young looked with cold disapproval at the two girls. "You're doing it all wrong," he said.

As if they had heard him, the fish vanished. A few quick lithe shadows shot under the boat and then were gone. The water was an oily green, a lettuce green, reaching down, down, into nothing. As Judy and Laurel turned to stare at him, David said, "You weren't throwing out enough bait. You let them get away."

"We didn't do badly," Judy said, looking at the dozen or more mackerel still flopping around in the bottom of the punt.

"You were so slow pulling your lines in that half of the fish got away."

"I wouldn't be surprised if they heard you coming," Laurel said sweetly. "That's why they went away."

[113]

It was a second before David caught her meaning; then a wave of red slowly spread under his freckles and out to the tips of his ears. He said, speaking to Judy not Laurel, "When I let you have my punt, I didn't know you were going to let someone else bang her around."

Laurel was looking for trouble, and she didn't give Judy a chance to answer. "Does this ratty little tub belong to you? I should think a big fisherman like you would have a decent boat. This thing rows like a log."

"I have got a decent boat," David shouted. "The *North Wind* is better than any of your dinky little sailboats that turn over if you sneeze. Even that punt is safer than any boat you've got."

Judy twisted the fishline between her fingers. She wished desperately that Laurel and David would not shout at one another so, but the quarrel was on in earnest. David was furious over the attack on his beloved boats, but Laurel

could say such biting things that it was hard
to answer her back.

"You've lived in a mudhole all your life,"
Laurel said. "You're as hard-shelled and stupid
as the lobsters you catch. What do you know
about boats? You never saw a real one."

David slammed his oars into the oarlocks.
"Just because you folks have got money you
don't boss the world, you know. And what did
a girl ever know about boats, anyway!" With
this he headed his skiff out of the cove and
never looked back at them again.

CHAPTER 9

The *North Wind*

It was clear that the day's fishing was ended. Laurel scattered more bait into the water and they threw out their lines hopefully, but the mackerel did not return. Neither Judy nor Laurel mentioned David, but the quarrel hung like a shadow over them.

In the end Laurel gave Judy all of the fish. "You might as well take them," she said. "No one at home will bother with them."

"Uncle Walter loves them," Judy said. "He salts them down for winter."

"He can have them," Laurel said. For some reason she seemed eager to get away. It was still early when they came ashore, but though Laurel had been full of fun until David had come along, now she was moody and silent. She seemed to want nothing except to go home.

"Shall I help you with the fish?" she asked, as Judy tied up the *Pant.* She didn't seem enthusiastic in making the offer, and when Judy said no, her uncle would want to clean them right here on the shore, Laurel looked relieved.

"I'll go home then," she said. "Mother'll be worrying about me. I've had a lot of fun and perhaps we can go again some time." But she did not say the words as if she really meant them.

When she had gone, Judy walked up to the bait house to get a basket for the mackerel. She pondered over Laurel's sudden change in mood and wondered if she had really enjoyed herself. They had been having wonderful fun up until the moment David appeared. But the quarrel between David and Laurel had left a hurt spot on her mind, even though she had not taken any part in it. She wondered if Laurel had been unhappy over it, too.

Boots crunched in the sand behind her, and Uncle Walter said, "Has your friend gone home?"

Judy turned gratefully at the sound of his voice. "Yes, and she gave me all of the fish, too. There must be two dozen of them. Can you salt them down?"

"Why, yes, I guess so," her uncle said. He began to take the slender, beautiful fish out of the bottom of the punt. "Didn't Laurel take any of them?"

"She said no one at home would want them."

"We should cook some of them and invite her over to dinner," Uncle Walter said, putting the last fish into the basket. "The child probably doesn't even know what fried mackerel tastes like. Did she have fun?"

"Oh, we had fun fishing. Mackerel bite so fast. They're certainly different from flounders."

"They can be lively when they're running well. What happened after you stopped fishing?"

Judy kicked her foot in the sand. "Nothing much." Uncle Walter said no more. He found a clean plank washed up by the sea and began splitting open the fish and cleaning them on it. As fast as he cleaned them he washed them in the clear salt water.

Judy watched the blood from the mackerel spread out and stain the water. Then she said, "David came fishing, too. Only the fish were gone by the time he got there. He didn't catch any."

"Did you give him some of yours?"

Judy shook her head. "Laurel and David had a row," she went on. "I wished they hadn't, not when I was around. It spoils everything."

"You can't keep people from quarreling, I guess," her uncle said, to comfort her. "You've quarreled with David yourself, you know."

"David is awfully rude," Judy said. "But then Laurel said such mean things to him. I don't know *which* side to take."

"Don't take either," her uncle advised. "You can't back friend against friend without getting hurt."

It sounded so easy but it wasn't, and Judy did not see how she could explain to her uncle what was really troubling her. David had been rude to both of them, but that hadn't surprised her. The things that Laurel had said, however, were much worse. Of course, she had been thinking of David when she spoke of living in a mudhole and of not knowing a decent boat when he saw one, but Judy could not keep back the feeling that these words had been in-

tended for her, too. Maybe Laurel thought she wasn't any smarter than David.

The fish were cleaned now and her uncle put them in the basket. As they started for home he began to talk about other things than David and Laurel. "We'll let your aunt fry some of these for supper, and then you can help me salt the rest of them down. And do you know, I think Kate's got baked apple with cream for dessert."

Soon the kitchen was filled with the wonderful smell of frying mackerel. Judy went down to the cellar and brought up the little earthen crock. Then her uncle showed her how to pack the rest of the fish into it and cover them with salt.

By suppertime Judy had forgotten her worries. When the dishes were washed and put away it was bedtime. Judy was used to going to bed early in the summer and rising early in the morning. Uncle Walter was always up before the sun, so he could haul the lobster traps before the day grew windy. From her bedroom window Judy looked down upon Aunt Kate's flower garden. The perfume of the flowers drifted up to her; the night was still and windless. In the east the full moon looked like a great purple-red bruise on the sky's face.

Judy felt a vague sadness as she remembered what had happened during the day, but the worry was gone. She was too sleepy to stay awake for long.

Judy woke because someone was moving about in the kitchen, which was right under her bedroom. She yawned; was it morning already? The bedroom window was a pale gray. It was much too early for even Uncle Walter to be up, but again she heard the clank of a stove cover downstairs.

Judy pulled her clothes on quickly. Even in the summer, it was cool enough in the early

morning to make her shiver and hurry with
her dressing. She ran down to the kitchen and
the warm wood stove.

The kitchen was bright with lights, and Aunt
Kate, still in her wrapper, was sleepily stirring
the fire. An empty coffee cup stood on the
table at her uncle's place, but Uncle Walter was
gone.

"Judy, did I wake you?" Aunt Kate asked in
surprise.

"What's wrong?" Judy asked. Her eyes blinked at the little clock on the wall. "It's only three o'clock," she said.

"There was no need for you to get up," her aunt said. "There's nothing you can do. David woke us up. His father wanted your uncle to help him. The *North Wind* is gone from her mooring. They don't know just what has happened; perhaps she's been stolen."

CHAPTER 10

The Missing Boat

Judy was heading for the wharf as fast as she could run. She had begged so hard that her aunt had not even made her wait and eat break-fast. If she was lucky enough she might catch up with her uncle and the Youngs, and per-haps they would let her go with them.

All the way she was thinking, So the *North Wind* has been stolen! But who would ever do such a thing? The *North Wind* was valuable, of course, but it was so large a boat that it would be impossible to hide it. If an alarm were sent to the Coast Guard they would almost certainly catch the thief.

The misty gray was growing lighter in the east. A gull circled the wharf with a harsh, lonesome cry. She heard the clink of metal on metal and the sound of men's voices. They came from Uncle Walter's old lobster boat, the *Alice*.

Judy scrambled down the stairway from the wharf to the float. She made a cup out of her hands and shouted into the mist. "Hi there!"

There was no answer and Judy shouted again. This time a man's voice called, "Who is it?"

"It's me, Judy. I want to go with you."

She heard David say, "We can't wait for her."

Then Uncle Walter called, "The *Pant* is there. Can you row out in her and be quick about it?"

"I'm coming. I'm coming," Judy answered.

She had to run back to the bait house on the shore to get the oars. The *Pant* was dripping with cold dew, and the knot in the wet rope was hard to untie. Judy struggled with it, expecting every moment to hear the *Alice's* engine start.

She was in the *Pant* and had started to row out into the mist when the engine coughed. Judy turned toward the sound and pulled hard. The *Alice* loomed up suddenly, right in front of her. "Here she is now," David's father said. "We'll leave the *Pant* at the mooring, Judy."

Soon afterward they were under way and headed out of the cove. The *Pant* had been left tied to the *Alice's* mooring, for they already had the skiff the men had rowed out in.

David had taken charge of the skiff, even though Judy usually did when she was aboard her uncle's boat. First he held the skiff close to the *Alice* to prevent the line from catching in the propeller, and then, as the boat picked up speed, he let the line out. The skiff tugged and pulled, leaping like a fish in the wake of the larger boat. When the skiff was a safe distance behind the *Alice,* David snubbed the line quickly around a cleat and then fastened it.

Judy knelt on the stern seat by his side. David had not spoken to her since she had come aboard, but Judy was so excited that she had not noticed this. "Do you think the *North Wind* was really stolen?" She had to shout to make herself heard above the roar of the engine.

"No," David shouted back. He looked at her oddly. "Don't you know what happened?" he asked. Judy stared at him and then he said, "Didn't your friend tell you what she was going to do?"

"My friend?"

"The one who knows so much. The summer girl," David yelled.

"Laurel? What did she do?"

"Something happened to the mooring line," David said darkly. "It was brand-new, so it couldn't have parted. Someone must have cut it."

"Well, it wasn't Laurel," Judy declared.

"She hated me," David said. "She wanted to get even with me."

"But to set a boat adrift. . . ." Judy objected.

"Didn't she ever say anything about doing something to the *North Wind?*"

Judy was silent. Against her will she remembered several things Laurel had said and done. What had Laurel said the day they cooked the crabs? Something about getting even with David and doing something to the *North Wind*. She remembered, too, Laurel's strange behavior after the last quarrel with David and her haste to get away.

"Even if she had wanted to she couldn't

[131]

have done it," Judy said at last. "How could she set the *North Wind* adrift?"

"What's so hard about that?" David asked. "Anyone who can row or use a knife could do it."

"But someone would have seen her," Judy objected.

"At night?"

Laurel had the skiff that went with the *Cheshire* and once she had told Judy that she often went rowing after dark. Her parents were used to it; they would not think it strange if she had taken it out last night.

"Does Uncle Walter think she did it?" Judy asked at last.

"He won't say and neither will Dad," David answered. "But *I* know who did it."

David did not say any more but climbed forward on the bow of the *Alice* with his father. Ordinarily Judy would have crawled up there with them, but now she remained where she was. Day was breaking. The sun came up blood red across the bay and the morning mist began to fade before it. Now they could see for a long distance.

The search for the *North Wind* was not wholly guesswork. They knew the direction of the wind and the tide when she had gone adrift, and so they went in the same direction now.

It was Mr. Young who shouted from his lookout in the bow. "There's something white in back of the Fiddler. Better have a look at it."

The Fiddler was a ledge that was just awash at high water. Now at half tide it looked like a long black streak. Uncle Walter swung the *Alice* in around it and they all strained their eyes. It was the *North Wind* all right, tipped up on one side.

Carried by the tide, she must have come up

on the ledge at high water and gone aground. As the tide ebbed away she had tipped over and now she lay on one side. The tide was flowing in again and this had partially righted her, although she still had a strong list to starboard.

Uncle Walter slowed the *Alice* to a crawl. David and his father came down off the bow, Mr. Young shaking his head. "She's listing bad," he said.

"Think she's hurt any?" Uncle Walter asked.

"Can't tell. Those rocks look mighty sharp." He began pulling the skiff in.

Uncle Walter let the engine idle and looked at the sky. "I don't like the weather. If it comes on to blow, you'll lose her for sure."

Mr. Young held the skiff while David scrambled into it. "We'll see how she looks inside. If she hasn't got a hole in her, we'll get her off quick as we can."

"*If* we can," Uncle Walter corrected. "And

we can't do anything until the tide comes in."

David and his father rowed toward the *North Wind*. Uncle Walter let the *Alice* idle along, keeping the engine running just enough to hold the boat up against the tide. Judy watched the skiff move in under the *North Wind's* starboard side and saw David and his father scramble aboard. "Do you think she's really a wreck?" Judy asked.

"I hope not." Her uncle sighed. "The Youngs didn't have much insurance on her. The *North Wind* cost them so much that they took a chance and slighted on that."

After a moment Judy said, "David thinks Laurel cut the *North Wind* adrift because she was mad at him."

"I know," her uncle answered. "David's terribly upset over it. He says Laurel threatened to hurt the boat. Did she ever say anything to you, Judy?"

Judy drew in a long breath. But just then a

shout came from the *North Wind*. Mr. Young was waving his arms to them. It was not easy to understand him with the engine going and the other boat so far away, but he managed to make clear that the *North Wind* had not suffered any serious damage so far. David was already climbing back into the skiff; his father was going to stay aboard the *North Wind*.

Uncle Walter swung the *Alice* about in a wide circle. "That's some help," he said. "Now if the tide only gets up before the wind does, we may get her off all in one piece." He had reason to be worried. Already in the east thin clouds spread out like the tails of galloping horses. The wind had freshened; it pushed against the *Alice* and tossed up little whitecaps.

Judy turned to look into the wind and caught her breath. Around the point of the Fiddler something white flashed—a sail. Then the *Cheshire*, already feeling the quickening wind, came racing into view.

"It's Laurel," Judy called to her uncle, and her heart sank. This was the worst time in the world for Laurel to turn up.

CHAPTER 11

Two Rescues

Uncle Walter had seen the sailboat too, and he was watching it uneasily. "She shouldn't have come out here," he said. "It's breezing up too much for that little boat."

By this time David had pulled up beside the *Alice.* "How is the *North Wind?*" Uncle Walter asked, turning to him.

"She doesn't seem to be hurt. She's not leaking any." He held on to the side of the *Alice.* "Dad wants to get a line out to her. He doesn't like the looks of the weather."

"I don't either," Uncle Walter said. "It's going to blow hard before too long. But I doubt if we can start her before the tide comes in more." He went below to look for the lines they would need.

David glanced at the sailboat that had now rounded the tip of the Fiddler. "I see your friend's coming to look at the damage she's caused," he said to Judy. "If she doesn't watch it, she'll be in trouble herself."

"Laurel knows how to handle a boat," Judy said. "And David, I think you're wrong. I don't believe she ever touched the *North Wind*."

"Of course, you wouldn't think so."

Judy ignored this. "Laurel loves boats. I don't believe she'd harm one just to get even with you."

Uncle Walter had appeared on deck with a stout hawser in his hands. "You can take this back to the *North Wind*," he said. "Tell your dad we'll give it a try, anyway." A squall of

wind made the *Alice* stagger. David caught hold of her side as the skiff swung out in the wind.

Judy shouted, "The sailboat! She's gone over!"

"Good heavens!" Uncle Walter exclaimed. The squall had caught the *Cheshire* just as it rounded the point. It had tipped over with startling speed as only a sailboat can. "Get aboard, David," Uncle Walter said. "Quick! And watch the skiff."

He was already turning the *Alice* toward the sailboat. David scrambled aboard and he and Judy fended the skiff away from the *Alice's* propeller.

"Laurel can swim," Judy said, mostly to quiet her own fear. "She'll be all right."

"If she didn't hit her head going over or get tangled up in the sail," David answered. "It was a fool thing, coming out in that little boat in this kind of weather."

They were up beside the *Cheshire* now and, sure enough, there was Laurel's head. She was holding on to the sailboat. "Good girl," Uncle Walter said with relief. "Stay with the boat."

"David," Uncle Walter said, "take the wheel. I've got to use the skiff. I can't get any closer."

"I can swim," Laurel shouted.

"You stay where you are," Uncle Walter

shouted back, but Laurel had started already. Uncle Walter swung the skiff out to meet her. "Thank heavens," he said, when Laurel caught hold of the skiff.

The *Alice* was so close and it was so hard to lift Laurel out of the water and into the skiff that Uncle Walter simply swung the skiff back to the larger boat. Then Laurel climbed up on his shoulders, and while he held the skiff close to the *Alice*, Judy helped her to scramble on board. Laurel looked more like a drowned cat than anything else. The water poured out of her shirt and her hair and her dungarees, and her teeth were chattering with the cold.

"Get that oilskin that's down in the cabin, Judy," Uncle Walter said. "That will keep her from feeling the wind."

"My boat!" These were Laurel's first words. "We've got to save my boat!"

"Look," David said, "we're not going to worry

over your boat. The wind's breezing up and we want to save mine." It was true; the wind was sending the whitecaps dancing.

"I'm sorry, Laurel," Uncle Walter said. "I can't salvage two wrecks at once. The *North Wind* is in more danger than your sailboat. Someone can pick her up later."

Judy had brought up the oilskin now and Laurel crawled into it. It was much too big for her and she wrapped it round and round herself. "I'm sorry I caused all this trouble," she said. "I know my sailing wasn't very good, and I should have watched out for that squall."

"And now we've lost time in getting the *North Wind* off," David said. "It's too bad you didn't stay wherever you came from."

Laurel perched up on the stern seat beside Judy. "What ails your friend?" she asked. "Does he growl all the time?"

Oh, dear, Judy thought. David calls her my friend and Laurel calls David my friend, and

[147]

they both do it to be sarcastic. Aloud she said, "David's worried over the *North Wind*."

"I know," Laurel said. "I went over to your house this morning and your aunt told me about it. Then I thought I would take the *Cheshire* and look for you. What ever happened?"

Judy was silent. She couldn't very well say, "Don't *you* know what happened?"

"She went adrift," Judy said at last, and felt more guilty than ever.

Laurel said smoothly, "What's the matter, Judy? Why are you so worried? They'll get her off, and besides, she doesn't belong to you."

"She belongs to my friends," Judy said coldly.

Uncle Walter had the *Alice* turned about now and had headed back to the *North Wind*. "It must be almost high water," he said to David. "We'll have to work fast."

David climbed into the skiff and started to carry the towline back to the *North Wind*. Uncle Walter sent Judy and Laurel up on the bow where they would be out of his way. They sat on the smooth rounded deck that covered the *Alice's* bow. Their feet were braced against the tiny rail that ran about its edge. Laurel had not given so much as another glance to her own boat, and she seemed delighted to be here watching the work on the *North Wind*. But Judy felt wretched.

As if she sensed the trouble, Laurel asked, "How did she happen to go adrift? I thought the Youngs were good sailors."

"Well," Judy said in an unhappy voice, "David thinks someone cut the mooring line."

Laurel understood then, but what shocked Judy the most was that she did not seem to be angry or even upset. She seemed to regard David's suspicions as a joke. "David must think I'm really good," she said, and began to laugh. "I never thought he'd give a girl the credit for being able to cut a boat adrift."

Aunt Kate is right, Judy thought. You can't

understand what they are thinking. Laurel should have been angry at being accused of such a thing or she should have been ashamed, but she shouldn't have laughed. "You could get into a lot of trouble if it was true," she said coldly.

Laurel glanced sideways at her. "So *you* believe it too. I thought this was just one of David's nightmares. What does your uncle think?"

"I don't know," Judy said. She knew that she should deny that she believed it. In spite of everything she did not believe that Laurel could be so mean, and yet the words wouldn't come. If only Laurel would *say* she didn't do it, Judy thought wretchedly. But Laurel said nothing.

David had reached the *North Wind* now. The tide had flowed in so that the boat was almost upright. The *Alice* moved slowly ahead, although the sea was running so high now that it was hard to hold the boat steady. The line between the two boats tightened. Would the *North Wind* move? It *must* move, Judy thought; they could not lose it now. She tried to make it move by sheer will power.

The *Alice* had been stopped dead. Even Laurel braced her feet hard against the railing in excitement. "She's got to move," she whispered, and Judy realized that Laurel, too, was trying to will it into moving.

Ever so little the *Alice* inched ahead. David and his father shouted; Uncle Walter waved his hand. The *North Wind* was free. She was rolling in the seas, but a few minutes later Mr. Young had the engine going and she was under her own power. The towline was taken in and the two boats ranged themselves side by side.

"Everything O.K.?" Uncle Walter shouted. "She leaking any?"

"A little," Mr. Young shouted back.

"Go on in," Uncle Walter yelled. "I'll pick the sailboat up." He shook his head at the Youngs' offer of help.

"You kids hang on up there and keep an eye out for the boat," he called up to Laurel and Judy. The *Cheshire* had drifted a long way with the wind and the tide. Finally Laurel caught sight of the white hull tossing in the seas.

"There it is!" she cried, pointing it out to Uncle Walter. As the *Alice* approached the sailboat, Laurel said, "My father will pay you for towing the *Cheshire* in."

"Your father ought to have a talking-to for ever letting you go out in that sailboat today," Uncle Walter answered. "If we hadn't seen you when you went over, you might have drowned."

"Dad didn't know anything about it," Laurel admitted. "I thought I could come out and help you hunt for the *North Wind*."

[152]

"Then you must have been worried, too, about her being adrift," Judy said. "That is, if you wanted to help find her."

"Why should I be worried?" Laurel asked. "Didn't I cut her adrift? I paddled out in the middle of the night and took the butcher knife —or was it the ax—"

"Oh, shut up!" Judy cried. "You know I never said I thought you did. But you don't have to act as if it was a joke."

"If you kids will stop fighting and watch this wheel," Uncle Walter interrupted, "I'll see if I can pick her up. You want to keep her headed straight into the wind, Judy."

Judy hung on to the spokes of the steering wheel while her uncle attempted to catch the *Cheshire* with the boat hook. Laurel, suddenly sober, tried to help him. "You can hand me that line," Uncle Walter said to her. "Watch it! You'll be overboard again."

It was really growing rough now. Judy's

stomach felt weak and fluttery, perhaps because she hadn't had any breakfast, but she didn't really feel hungry. She felt as if she would be much happier back in the quiet water of the cove.

They had a towline on the *Cheshire* at last. There would be no time to right her out here in the rough water. She would be towed home behind the *Alice,* an upside-down tangle of canvas, rope, and wood.

Because the *Cheshire* was hard to tow, it was almost noon by the time the *Alice* got back to Young's Cove. The *North Wind* was tied to the *Alice's* mooring, and David and his father were using the *Pant* to locate the other mooring, which had dropped from sight because of the accident.

The *North Wind's* mooring consisted of a wooden buoy, a line attached to a chain, and a block of granite, which rested on the bottom. When the boat was in use, the buoy held up the line and chain and marked the location of the mooring. When the boat was moored, the buoy was picked up with a boat hook and the line was tied to the bow of the boat. Since the line had parted from the chain, however, the buoy and line were left on the *North Wind* and the chain had dropped to the bottom. Ever since they had returned, the Youngs had been dragging a grapple over the spot, trying to pick up the chain.

"They've found it," Uncle Walter said. Judy could see now that the Youngs had something in the skiff and that they were tying a new line and buoy onto it. She wondered, now that they had found the mooring, if it would be possible to tell what had happened. Perhaps they would never really know. Laurel, by her side, seemed as unconcerned as ever.

Uncle Walter came up beside them. "We'll swap moorings," he said. "What happened?"

David said nothing, but his father lifted the

chain a little. "One of those things you never expect to happen. There's a nick in this chain and it made a rough spot. Somehow the line got under it. The last time we picked the mooring up the line must have caught in the spot and, with the tide pulling against it, it was chewed right through. A puff of wind, and a tug from the boat was enough to part it."

"Things go wrong even when you're careful," Uncle Walter agreed. "If you've got that mooring fixed, will you give me a hand? I've got to beach this sailboat, or what's left of her."

David and his father climbed aboard the *Alice*. While the men were busy with the sailboat, David, Judy, and Laurel were alone on the bow. David was clearly embarrassed. He scratched his ear and ran his fingers through his hair. Judy felt so sorry for him that she looked the other way, but Laurel smiled sweetly at him.

"Well," David began, "I'm sorry I said the

[156]

things I did. I guess I was just mad. I see now they weren't true." He looked around at Judy as if hoping for some help.

"Of course you're sorry," Laurel said very nicely. "And it's perfectly all right. I don't mind a bit being accused of wrecking a boat. You're sorry for all the other things you said about me, too, aren't you?" she added.

"Well, yes." David began to squirm. "I mean. . . . Laurel, I really do feel like a skunk." His voice trailed off.

The wicked little grin came back to Laurel's face. "It's worth being called a criminal to hear that," she said.

"Oh, please!" Judy cried. "Don't start fighting again! I told you, David, that she would never do it."

"Good for you, Judy!" Laurel laughed and put an arm about Judy's shoulder. Judy thought, Aunt Kate is right. I shall never understand her, but does it matter? David didn't understand Laurel either, but he had said he was sorry and he had meant it. That was all that mattered right now.

"Come on, Laurel," she said. "While they're beaching the *Cheshire* let's go up to my house and get some dry clothes and some breakfast."